EDGES

One Foot Under

Book 3

Bjorn Esterday Was Not Born Yesterday

Wynter Sommers

GJ dePillis

Published by Pure Force Enterprises, Inc.
California, USA
Since 2002

ISBN-13: 978-1-7184-0004-7
ISBN-10: 1-7184-0004-7

Bjorn Series Alternate Reading Plan

1st   Edges Book 1
2nd   Edges Book 2
3rd   Gone Book 1
4th   Firebrand Book 1
5th   Edges Book 3
6th   Firebrand Book 2
7th   Gone Book 2
8th   Gone Book 3
9th   Firebrand Book 3
10th Gone Book 4
11th Firebrand Book 4
12th Gone Book 5
13th Gone Book 6
14th Edges Book 4
15th Firebrand Book 5
16th Gone Book 7
17th Firebrand Book 6
18th Gone Book 8
19th Firebrand Book 7
20th Gone Book 9
21st Firebrand Book 8
22nd Gone Book 10
23rd Gone Book 11
24th Gone Book 12
25th Gone Book 13
26th Firebrand Book 9 (End)
27th Gone Book 14
28th Gone Book 15
29th Gone Book 16
30th Gone Book 17
31st Gone Book 18 (End)
32nd Edges Book 5
33rd Edges Book 6
34th Edges Book 7
35th Edges Book 8
36th Edges Book 9 (End)

Main Characters

- **Sarah Paradise** - School Teacher
- **Bjorn Esterday** - Reporter at the Daily Memo Newspaper. Works for Sammy Scribe.
- **Percy Snatcher** - Head of the AnCor para-military cell
- **Slash** - Loyal AnCor follower of Percy
- **Noah Lantz** - Earth Farmer husband to Ruth Lantz
- **Joshua Lantz** - Earth Farmer child of Ruth and Noah Lantz
- **Ruth Lantz** - Earth Farmer Mother to Joshua. Wife to Noah. Expert quilter.
- **Jack Courtly** - Head of Courtly City
- **Queenie Courtly** -Wife to Jack Courtly
- **Ace Courtly** - Child of Jack and Queenie Courtly
- **Skipper Courtly** - Brother to Jack Courtly
- **Pip Courtly** - Child of Skipper Courtly
- **Widow Medicina**- Courtly City citizen and train passenger, recently widowed.
- **Mrs Libris** - Librarian

Characters (continued)

- **Train** passengers
- **Soldier** Police aka SPs
- **Soldier Police Officer Guard** Gene
- **AntiCorporatists** aka AnCors
- **Library** patrons
- **Sammy Scribe** Bjorn's editor
- **Workers** at Courtly mail office
- **Summer students** at Courtly Offices
- **Attorney** Atushi

CONTENTS

ACKNOWLEDGMENTS

To all those gentle souls who have graciously given tokens of love, hope, and kind considerations to others.

0 Preface

Last time, Jack was on the Courtly train ordering a first-class meal for the Lantz family as a thank you for taking care of Ace. Jack's plans are interrupted when an AnCor silently slips aboard the train and threatens to murder Noah Lantz. Jack takes a bullet for the Earth Farmer and the train passengers are taken hostage. The remaining AnCors board the train and take it over, a very bold move as the train seems to continue travelling uninterrupted..

In an effort to protect the passengers and the Courtly family, Guard Gene, an SP, is injured and unable to further resist the well-coordinated AnCor Attack.

1 CHAPTER Year 2030: Execution (Continuous Ch 26)

Outside the captured train which had now halted, the weather was ironically pleasant. It would have been a nice day for a picnic if it weren't for the shrieking AnCors who were now roughly herding terrified passengers off the train.

Back on the train, crouched inside a closet, Mrs. Queenie Courtly waited for silence in her hiding place. She held her breath, not wanting to make a sound, carefully listening to make sure she heard none. After a long moment, she slowly eased open the door, crept out and quietly closed the door behind her.

1

Still cautious, she tip-toed to the dining compartment where only moments earlier she realized her husband had been shot by a waiter.

Her hand gently touched the door. It whooshed opened suddenly, causing her to gasp in surprise. Seeing the dining car was unoccupied, trembling, she slipped inside to look around.

Where was her husband? Was he only injured and now was outside with the other passengers?

Queenie crept to a window and, careful not to be seen herself, looked outside scanning the dusty tear-strewn faces of the passengers.

She didn't see Jack.

On the floor was a large blood stain, which she assumed was Jack's, her beloved husband.

She now stood, looking at the room. A mess. A shame. Why would they do this to innocents? Then, she saw a body.

Queenie noticed the man was wearing

a Courtly uniform. This man was a Soldier Police. Blood on his hands and face caused Queenie to feel faint. When she turned, her eyes filling with tears of distress, she did not notice that this corporation soldier had twitched, then returned to his motionless state.

Distressed that she couldn't find her husband, Queenie realized she was faced with a dilemma in which she was armed with nothing but her good manners.

Queenie, overwhelmed by feelings of uselessness and helplessness, uncertain about what to do, was abruptly thrown to her knees as the train lurched forward.

Queenie realized the train had been attacked, then abandoned, but she didn't think these AnCors would actually try to take the train itself.

What possible use could it be?

She tried to figure things out as she regained her balance. It could only run on tracks owned by Courtly and other Corporations. Eventually, these AnCors would be overtaken by Soldier Police from either Courtly or those other Corporations owning the tracks.

All logic dissipated as Queenie stopped breathing to hear approaching footsteps and conversation through the walls of the dining car. She made her way silently to the opposite side of the dining car to exit.

As she opened the door to escape, she ran straight into the arms of an AnCor, who smiled, deftly grabbed her arms and pulled the train emergency stop cord.

The train groaned to a halt.

Queenie was escorted out roughly and walked the thirty feet they had travelled back toward the huddled group of passengers. They were standing in a line along the edge of a ditch that had been obviously dug out by the AnCors sometime earlier in preparation for their attack at this place.

Queenie realized none of the AnCors had bothered hiding their faces. Once she saw the ditch, she understood they didn't care if the passengers knew their identity because all these witnesses would soon be silenced and dumped into that yawning makeshift grave.

Queenie was brusquely shoved toward a group near the end of a lineup. Never before had she been so happy to see a familiar face. She accepted the hand of the befuddled Widow Medicina.

Queenie thought the widow reached out to Queenie for comfort during their final moments, but she saw now that the widow was trembling uncontrollably, losing her balance, terrified.

The wind started to pick up, hissing ominously. Blasts of sand hit Queenie's face causing her to squint at the sting of dust in her eyes. She blinked a bit and noticed two scraps of fabric. Twelve inch squares of a quilting pattern loosely stitched together floated on the currents of the wind.

Instantly, she recognized the scraps as the pattern she had created for Ace's quilt. It seemed so long ago when Ruth Lantz had shown her that piece of fabric.

In the distance, Queenie saw small dark boulders scattered about. When the dust cleared for a moment, she saw more clearly that those boulders were actually the bodies of former passengers.

Her heart sank. She realized she was the last one alive in her group who had started this family adventure so happily. She smiled to herself remembering how earlier that day the subtle shade of a hat was so important and all-absorbing.

Now her world was just her and the Widow Medicina.

A spray of bullets shot out, catching the attention of the hostages. One AnCor was using the floating quilting squares as target practice. Somebody shouted at him to conserve the bullets as they were needed for the hostages.

The wind picked up the quilting squares and floated them out of range. This was a small comfort for Queenie, who felt that her soul would soon be safe in heaven, escaping this horrific nightmare. Even their bullets couldn't separate the edges of her quilt, and

Queenie was hoping the scraps would float away to safety.

A grunt emanated from the train engine as it started up again. Some of the AnCors jumped on board, leaving a couple of executioners behind. As other AnCors ran to catch the moving train, they shouted back to the executioners to hurry and join them.

Another wave of bullets tat-a-tat-a-tatted out.

The Widow Medicina clutched for her chest with her right arm. Queenie felt the widow's left hand grow limp, as the older woman gasped. Widow Medicina was suffering a heart attack.

"Stay calm, Widow Medicina, please. Dear God in Heaven. Help!" Queenie whispered to herself as she squeezed her eyes shut. The widow now lost her footing, dragging Queenie down into the ditch, and then tumbling on top of her.

The AnCors, satisfied that their job was done, and all the hostages were now dead in the ditch, raced to haul themselves onboard the caboose.

One AnCor, standing on the caboose platform, braced himself against the rail of the retreating train, and shot one last spray at the collapsed heap of bodies in the ditch.

A soft gust of wind lifted the quilt squares, now laced with bullet holes, to land on top of the final resting place of now motionless hostages.

The cheers of the victorious AnCors faded as the Courtly Dynamics Train chugged away.

2 CHAPTER Year2030: One Week Before the Train Leaves (Continuous Ch 27)

The executive office of Jack Courtly at Courtly Dynamics Corporation was decorated with simple understated elegance. There were no glass knick-knacks and no self-aggrandizing trophies. The bookshelves held practical technical manuals and well-used reference materials.

Both Courtly brothers stood in the middle of the office, faces red from arguing.

"It's for the good of the company,

9

Jack!" Skipper shook his head at his giggledsomething happens to you. Signing this protects everyone. It's insurance."

"If I sign that, Skip, my wife and child don't get a dime. You created this... this... Mayfounder Foundation as a phony charity! Queenie raises money for genuine causes. Not some shell of a..." Jack choked on his words.

"Attorney Atsushi is the one who legally structured Mayfounder to be more than just some charity. It also does research." Skipper grabbed a piece of paper from Jack's desk, adjusted his glasses, and read, struggling with each syllable, "...to direct nanoparticles to specific organs for targeted medicinal analysis, replication, and delivery..."

"Really?" Jack protested in disbelief, "A lawyer wrote that?" Jack scoffed, "If Mayfounder is the beneficiary of my will, then that means YOU get everything, Skip. Am I right? Why can't you do business even somewhat ethically? Have you totally forgotten everything that Dad taught us?"

"Don't bring Dad into this, Jack," warned Skipper. "He was a broken record with that Proverbs 3:27 nonsense."

"Oh, you mean...Do not withhold good...from those who trust you...?" Jack taunted. "Dad built this business based on that." Jack turned away from Skipper, too disgusted to even look at him.

"It's a greeting card," Skipper persisted, "...it is not profitable business advice." Then, raising his voice, Skipper blurted, "I can't believe Dad made you solely in charge of this place and not me. I'm the oldest! I should be in charge!"

Skipper slammed his hand down on Jack's desk on top of the paper he wanted Jack to sign. He took a deep slow breath, picked up the paper, and walked over to Jack with a smile. With a soothing voice Skipper said, "Herc. Just read it when you're more relaxed."

"You are totally blind to the consequences of this bad..." Jack snapped then checked himself to regain control.

"Read it," Skipper cooed, "You'll see its progress. It means more money for the business. For you, for Queenie, for Ace..."

Something in Jack cracked his cool exterior. "More Money? Skip, we've just pioneered a hugely profitable agreement with the Earth Farmers. It's legal and it's going to be especially lucrative. We don't need to saddle ourselves with this Mayfounder absurdity."

"Not 'we', Jack, 'you' did that. Throwing perfectly good money and land away on those Earthies." Skipper's lips slid into a wolfish snarl.

"We'll be opening a new fresh food division," Jack insisted, "and providing consistent, uncontaminated Earth Farmer grown produce to the people. Other corporate territories are already clamoring to trade with us. We'll make more money ethically than with your Mayfounder garbage."

Skipper interrupted, "You haven't even read..."

Jack cut him off, "I did read this, Skip, the first time you gave it to me." Jack clutched the papers in his hand, crumpling them, "I saw how this agreement also makes all Courtly businesses collaborate with organizations that have more ecological violations than...."

"..You are over reacting, Baby Boy." Skipper interrupted through clenched teeth.

"Don't patronize me!" Jack shoved the papers back at Skipper, who started to smooth out the wrinkles. "I don't want Courtly Corp's reputation tainted by Mayfounder pollution and all their unscientific lab experiments. I mean who knows what poison is really brewing in their kitchens."

Jack stopped himself abruptly. Slowly, he started again as if he was realizing something for the first time, "You already sealed this deal, didn't you?"

His eyes traced Skippers quivering lips as Jack continued with deliberation, "Older brother or not, you have no authority to enter any contractual agreement with any entity without me! You went ahead and brokered an agreement expecting ME to bail you out. You assumed I'd blindly sign if it crossed my desk. You didn't realize I actually read before I sign anything? You never thought about the consequences of agreeing on behalf of Courtly, did you?"

Shocked that he'd been so quickly discovered, Skipper Courtly tried to diminish the damage.

"Calm down, Jackie boy. Don't blow it all out of proportion. It's not like that. I mean it may seem a little like... Huh. I mean. You see. But. Jack, it's a lot of money." Skipper shrugged with his palms upward indicating that he was helpless to refuse.

Jack sneered in disgust as he gathered his belongings and headed toward the door, "I can't believe you hit me with this right before I'm scheduled to leave on a family holiday."

He put on his hat as he reached for the door, then turned back to Skipper, "You were at the speech I gave today giving all employees extra vacation hours to set an honorable example about priorities, and you just blew Courtly integrity out of the water with this stunt."

"Be reasonable. Mayfounder will develop products we can profit from," Skip countered. "That's integrity."

Jack walked back to his desk, grabbed the contract and threw it into his briefcase, "I'm keeping this to make sure you don't get your hands on it, Skipper Courtly. And I'm not signing it. I am not consenting to any variation of this. It's bad business."

Skipper bowed his head humbly, "I understand, Jack. And you've clearly made your position known."

Jack opened the door, then turned to Skipper, "Mayfounder Foundation? What a joke!"

"Jack, I respect your decision and won't bring it up again. I'm sorry." Skipper stood slump shouldered, with both eyes closed, as if in surrender to Jack.

Without answering, Jack stormed out.

After a moment, Skipper opened one eye, saw Jack's spacious office was empty, and then stepped toward the door to close it quietly. He scurried back to Jack's desk, sitting in Jack's simple leather chair. Out from a folder, Skipper produced another copy of the Mayfounder Foundation contract.

Skipper glanced at the floating holographic image, on Jack's desk, of Queenie and Jack together smiling. He wrinkled his nose and turned the image off. Then, Skipper took this new copy of the Mayfounder contract and turned to the unsigned blank signature page.

He picked up another document from Jack's desk of something else Jack had signed and put the signed document underneath the Mayfounder signature page.

Slowly, Skipper traced the signature, while glancing nervously up at the door, hoping nobody would need to enter. When completed, he held the original signature and the traced signature up to the light to make sure they basically matched.

Skipper made one more final adjustment to the signatures. Then tension melted from his forehead.

Good enough.

Who would dare doubt the authority of a Courtly, anyway. He crossed the room and opened up the door a little bit, while blowing confidently on the drying ink. Content, he sat down again and waited.

A few minutes later, a smart suited man knocked on the door. He adjusted his visitor badge as he walked in, not seeing who was inside the room.

"Sorry I'm late. Mr. Courtly," apologized Attorney Atushi. "Your security procedures for who can get in the building are annoyingly thorough." He looked up and saw Skipper, "Oh, I was expecting to meet Jack Courtly. Where is he?"

"Yes, yes, yes... he had to leave. Family emergency, but I stayed behind because he really wanted to make sure that your law firm got this personally delivered."

Skipper handed over the freshly forged Mayfounder Foundation contract.

"It's not like him to miss an appointment. I mean he called my secretary personally, so I assumed it was urgent...." Attorney Atsushi said, more to himself than to Skipper, as he accepted the contract and took a moment to glance through it.

"Who drew this up?" he muttered to Skip as he kept reading.

"Oh, I don't know. Jack found some obscure lawyer someplace. I'm simply the messenger, Attorney Atsushi."

"It's just that Mr. Courtly's current will leaves his estate to his family...wife and child... and some to his domestic staff, charity, educational institutions. I'd have to look at it more closely, but it seems that this leaves everything to something called the Mayfounder Foundation. I've never heard of the Mayfounder Foundation," the lawyer explained.

"Y'know, Atsushi, instead of being a visitor all the time with that lawfirm, maybe you should think about becoming a full time employee at Courtly, here. Rumor has it that a rare and lucrative opportunity is opening up very soon."

Attorney Atsushi looked at Skipper for a long moment. Then he crossed over to Jack's desk and moved some papers around until he saw one with Jack's familiar signature on it.

Atsushi picked it up and held the signature next to the Mayfounder contract, comparing the swoops of the penmanship. The signature from Jack's desk looked genuine, whereas the Mayfounder signature looked traced with ink pooling in spots where the pen had hesitated.

Without a word, Atsushi looked at Skipper.

"Jack loves the Mayfounder Foundation," Skipper stammered to fill in the silence. "You see, only the day-to-day business is left in my care. Ace is too young and Jack's wife...I mean we all love Queenie, but she couldn't survive the stampede from a sale at a boutique let alone have the smarts to run a business. Poor thing. She's no survivor."

Skipper put an avuncular hand on Atsushi's shoulder as he continued, "I strongly feel Courtly Dynamics Corporation has an obligation to the stockholders. I mean, we don't want to sack Courtly employees in the unlikely event that something bad would happen to Jack, do we? Staff reductions would impact you, also, Mr. Atsushi. However, with this," Skipper indicated the contract Atsushi was holding, "...if Jack dies, the Mayfounder Foundation will provide funds from his estate to run the company and keep the employees working..."

Attorney Atsushi paused a long moment as Skipper's words trailed off.

Then the attorney spoke, "So, what you are saying is Jack Courtly never made this appointment with me. You did."

Atsushi thumbed through the contract, "And what you are really asking me to do is file this document to replace Jack Courtly's current beneficiaries in his will with the Mayfounder Foundation. Am I understanding the whole picture, Mr. Courtly ...Uh ...Skipper?"

3 CHAPTER Year 2036: Sarah Needs to Bring Something (Continuous Ch 28)

"Am I understanding the whole picture?" the reporter asked.

Skipper did not reply.

"Mr. Courtly?" Bjorn prompted, "About your castle? Did I get all the relevant renovation details?"

Skipper interrupted and ordered, "Mr. Reporter, whatever your name is, meet me in an hour at Courtly Corp. One hour!"

Skipper Courtly scrambled down the steps leading to his throne, and walked out.

As Skipper made his way through the main entrance of the very busy Courtly Corporate headquarters, he remembered back to that day in the past when he had stood arguing with his brother Jack for the last time, back in the Courtly corporate offices six years earlier.

How different the offices looked today. His son, Pip, now used his brother Jack's chair and desk. No reference manuals were to be found on any bookshelves.

Pip Courtly strolled into his executive office, which was cluttered with knick-knacks, and hand-blown object d'art, blobs of glass, all created by Pip, displayed on every shelf.

Pip wondered why his father Skipper was standing in the office motionless next to the wall of Pip's awards. Pip had encouraged other departments in the corporation to bestow numerous trophies upon Pip himself, to celebrate Pip's own excellence.

Bjorn Esterday, who was wearing a

"visitor" badge, was trying to get the attention of a glassy-eyed Skipper Courtly.

"Mr. Courtly?" Bjorn asked again. Then he looked over at Pip.

Pip found the expression on his father's face odd.

"You're still interviewing Dad?" Pip quipped to Bjorn.

Skipper was snapped back to the present day with Pip's comment and addressed Pip, "We've just come from the castle."

Then, turning to Bjorn, Skipper continued, "You've made plenty of notes to hold you for a while and I'm exhausted. My schedule simply won't allow more time for you today. Please see my secretary outside to schedule a time when I can take you on a private tour of our facilities and continue our interview. Oh, and remember to schedule your next visit at the castle."

"Thank you, Sir. Touring the offices will

add dimension to the series on your remodeling project and I'm sure the Lifestyle articles will generate more fans." Bjorn smiled and then walked to the door of the executive office, opened it, announced quietly, "I'll show myself out. Thank you, gentlemen."

Pip watched Bjorn leave, closing the door behind him.

Pip Courtly picked up a glass knick-knack and fiddled with it now that he was alone with his father, "Dad..." He started, "I have an idea..."

Skipper snapped back, "You have money! You don't need ideas!"

"But, Dad," Pip persisted, "I have an idea about the workers...

His father gave Pip a sardonic look. "Such as?"

"Make everybody change jobs to keep the workers interested."

"You mean 'cross-training'?" Skipper clarified.

"I don't know what to call it. I just made it up. I'm in charge. I'm supposed to have ideas." Pip pointed to his wall of awards.

"Pip, listen to me. You only need two skills. One, how to hold on to the money you have. Two, how to get even more money. Ideas are what you buy from other people."

Skipper shook his head as if perplexed why his son would miss such a simple lesson. Pip noted his father was looking very haggard. The many lines on his sullen face betrayed a life of self-indulgence.

Flopping onto a sofa in the office, Pip realized it was useless to press the point. He wanted to present a plan to improve morale at the plant so that the workers would be internally motivated to do a better job. It might even improve productivity if the workers weren't so disgruntled all the time. Driving them with threats was becoming less and less effective. But, Pip knew when to stop talking about work and changed the subject.

"So, what do you want to do, now?" Pip asked.

"I don't know, What do you normally do during the work day?" Skipper replied

"Um." Pip thought for a moment, "Not much. You feel like having some ice cream?"

Just outside the corner executive office, Bjorn wended his way to Sarah's desk. She looked up, surprised to see him.

"What are you doing here, Bjorn?"

She glanced around to make sure she wasn't heard and nobody was watching. "I never told the Courtly family that I know you. Can we talk later? We are still having dinner, tonight, right?"

"Yeah." Bjorn leaned in to whisper to Sarah, "We're still on for dinner tonight, but... I need you to bring me something..."

4 CHAPTER Year 2030: Camp AnCor (Continuous Ch 29)

The Anti-Corporatist camp was a haphazard maze of cloth tents and open camp fires. Only a couple of structures, built decades ago and obviously condemned and abandoned, were now taken over by the AnCors and served as offices to the much higher ranks in the group. This included men like Percy Snatcher.

With the train hi-jacking still fresh in his memory, Percy was off to a corner angrily discussing the play-by-play of how the operation had gone. He was unaware that across the room, a sloppily bandaged Jack Courtly was regaining consciousness.

"You mean you saw her and you did NOT take her as prisoner?" Percy hissed clutching the newspaper photo he had confiscated on the train. The blood-splattered, stepped-on photo showed Jack with his wife Queenie. "You shot all of them, left them there and didn't even check to see if one of them was her?"

The AnCor stammered, "I was being tidy. They fell in the ditch like you wanted...I never saw that picture til now, Mr. Snatcher."

"When will you learn which witnesses to kill, which to ransom, and which to sell as slaves. She could have been worth... Never mind! You'd just go around drilling everyone until they looked like Swiss cheese."

Percy heard Jack stirring. He unceremoniously ordered the AnCor, "Get out!"

The AnCor darted out of the room. Percy Snatcher walked deliberately to Jack, then looked down at him as one observes a frog before taking a scalpel and making the first cut for dissecting it.

Jack struggled to blink as he tried to break the seal of dried blood cementing his lashes together. He realized his hands were bound.

"Welcome to my humble abode, Mr. Jack Courtly, sir," Percy mocked with a sweeping exaggerated bow. "Thank you for helping us fight for freedom against your oppressive corporate regimes." He chuckled at his own irony.

"I don't understand. This is some employee dispute?" Jack was confused.

"No. This is a way of life for us, Jack. I may call you that, right?" Percy smiled. "You see, we don't do this part time after five o'clock, Jack. I hate money. I hate that I need it so desperately. I hate the things I have to do to get it. We need money to keep us living like this," Percy gestured with a sweeping arm to mockingly indicate the lack of grandeur of the AnCor camp, "...and that's why I had to keep you alive... You are now part of our inventory and we shall make a profit from selling you."

"Anybody at my office will pay whatever ransom you want. I can tell you whom to contact. My brother Mr. Skipper..."

"That's just it, Jack," Percy pulled up a broken-legged chair and sat close to Jack. "I did call. And I got to chat with Skippie."

"And?" asked Jack confident that Percy would tell him he'd be free soon. Jack struggled to sit up.

Percy took a deep breath before replying, "You corporatists love money more than life itself. It seems, Jack, that your brother, Skipper Courtly, will pay dearly. But, before he pays me, Jack, he requires proof of ...death, not life."

"I don't understand," Jack winced at

the pain as he moved unable to believe what he just heard. "Am I your hostage or are you going to kill me?"

5 CHAPTER- Year 2030: Mass Grave (Continuous Ch 30)

Only the whisper of a gentle breeze could be heard. One bird of prey flew in lazy circles high above the ditch at the side of the railroad tracks. Bodies, which had earlier trembled before the angry AnCors, now lay motionless.

The ditch was about two feet deep, two feet wide, and ten feet long. The AnCors had dug it hurriedly and had planned to cover up the bodies, but ran out of time, so the corpses lay exposed to the warm sun as food for scavengers.

At one end of the pile of carnage was the limp form of Widow Medicina, who was not shot, but had died of a sudden heart attack.

33

From underneath the weight of Widow Medicina, a disoriented searching hand stretched out tentatively. That hand then reached around to push off the older woman's heavy corpse.

Queenie Courtly had been shielded by the mass of the widow's body, but the force of the fall had caused Queenie's head to strike against a rock. Touching the wet viscose blood dripping from her own head, Queenie, confused, made feeble movements. She saw the bodies around her and gasped in horror.

Repelled by the sight, but seeing some movement, Queenie called out to those in the mass grave.

"Hello? Is everybody all right?"

She was greeted with silence, then realized that the motion she had seen was that of a bird tugging at a morsel of flesh. It squawked, then flew away.

Queenie crawled slowly and painfully, pulling herself up out of the shallow ditch, repeatedly apologizing as she stepped on hands and limbs. Queenie stumbled as she got to her feet. Dizzy, she made her way around the perimeter of motionless bodies, kneeling down from time to time to shake this individual or that one.

"Hello? Anybody? Do you know where this place is?" Frustrated, she called loudly, "Can anybody help me? Anyone hear me?"

She waited.

She listened.

She heard only the scurrying of small animals and the wind.

Eventually, she realized that she was completely alone.

Now what?

She saw a couple of fabric quilt squares loosely stitched together, fluttering on a nearby bramble bush. She reached in and, pricking her finger on a brier, freed the fabric from a thorny branch. She wiped the blood from her finger, and then her forehead, with the cloth. Then, as one would do with a handkerchief, she folded it loosely and tucked it into her pocket.

Turning around, squinting at the sun, the sky, the seemingly endless horizons, Queenie didn't know which way to go.

She stumbled around, uncertain.

In the distance, she saw something laying on the dirt. She walked over to it and picked it up. It was a jacket. Probably would fit a 12 year old, she reasoned. There was blood on it. She held it a long moment as if it should mean something to her, but she couldn't figure out why a youth-sized jacket covered in blood should mean anything.

Queenie couldn't remember that Ace had worn that jacket on the train.

Absentmindedly, she dropped the jacket.

It meant nothing.

She may not know what to do, but she did know she couldn't stay in this place.

Her ears picked up a rhythmic sound

in the distance. She headed toward the noise.

"There must be a road nearby," she whispered to herself.

Confused and exhausted, Queenie stumbled forward until she saw wild vegetation trampled down into a path.

She walked along it for a while. Her tongue was dry, making it difficult to swallow. Trickles of sweat dripped down her chest and back. She wiped her brow with the quilt squares she had tucked away earlier and then replaced the cloth, now damp with sweat and blood, back into her pocket.

She licked her lips. They stung and felt flaky and raw. With each step, her feet grew more painful. She felt blisters begin to form from the chaffing of sweaty feet in shoes that were never meant to touch rough earth.

Presently, she heard sounds of a crude wooden cart and horse hooves clopping along. The sounds seemed to be getting louder as if approaching her on this path.

Soon, within her view, Queenie saw a worn, horse drawn cart with three Earth Farmer men riding along. The cart halted with a "whoa" and one man hopped out gingerly approaching Queenie.

"Ma'am. Are you all right?" Elder James asked. He took note of her designer clothing, but also saw she was wounded and disoriented. Queenie couldn't really see him. Everything kept going in and out of focus for her.

"Not OK," Queenie stammered out. "Something happened. Accident. I think... Everyone..." Queenie sank to the ground.

The other two Earth Farmers jumped out of the cart and ran to her. One looked nervously up and down the path, vigilantly scouting to see if they could see if anybody else was in need of assistance. They didn't realize Queenie had walked quite a ways from the accident site.

Elder James spoke clearly and loudly, now.

"Ma'am. What is your name? Ma'am, don't you realize this is rebel country. AnCors travel through here. It is not safe for a woman to travel by herself."

Realizing the woman was unable to respond to him, Elder James turned to his two companions, "She must have encountered those bandits on her way to the widow's community and they must have stolen her belongings." He looked at her left hand and saw a wedding band. "Quickly, we must take her to the Widow's Cloister Infirmary."

The two men agreed and one rushed back to the cart pushing meager food supplies aside to make room for this new passenger. Elder James and the other Earth Farmer, picked up Queenie and placed her in the cramped cart as gently as they could.

"Is she suffering from shock?" One brother asked in hushed tones.

The last thing Queenie remembered about this rescue was the sight of a bunch of carrots tied together in front of her. As her eyes closed, one of the brothers removed his own cloak and covered this new passenger to keep her warm.

"Elder James, I fear if we are to bring this woman to the Widow's Cloister, then we shall have to delay our passage to the hungry prisoners."

"You are correct, sir. We must ensure this woman gets proper care. If we hurry, we may be able to first deliver her to safety, and then still make it to drop off the food to the prisoners. Let us recite Psalm 91 for our protection, Brothers."

The three men started the cart, steering their horse off the path they were travelling on, to head in another direction. For miles, nothing but wilderness surrounded them. Their wooden wheels plodded through the wild grasses, which caught into their spokes, slowing them down.

"Brother, what if we cannot arrive at the Cloister, nor the prison, nor return home before dark?"

"You are correct, Brother," the other

Earth Farmer stated. "We must ask God Almighty to protect us and guide us."

As the sun began to set, the men chanted in unison.

"He that dwelleth in the secret place of the most High shall abide under the shadow of the Almighty. I will say of the Everliving God, He is my refuge and my fortress: my God; in Him will I trust. Surely He shall deliver thee..."

The wheels of their cart creaked and strained as they rattled over rocky terrain and churned against the tall vegetation.

They continued, "... His truth shall be thy shield.... Thou shalt not be afraid for the terror by night; nor for the arrow that flies by day; ...nor for the destruction that wastes at noon. A thousand shall fall at thy side, and ten thousand at thy right hand; but it shall not harm thee..."

One Earth Farmer looked at Queenie and motioned to his companion that she seemed limp. With only his expression, he indicated his fear of Queenie's life slipping away.

The other reached over and felt for a pulse on Queenie's wrist. Yes. He found it. Queenie was still alive. Barely. They continued to chant.

"... There shall no evil befall thee, For He shall give His angels charge over thee, to keep thee in all thy ways....."

The three men exchanged worried glances as their horse trudged on. They were losing daylight and they still could not see their destination.

6 CHAPTER 2030: Welcome Back, Slash (Continuous Ch 31)

Disheveled and looking more worn than usual, Slash stumbled into the AnCor camp, barging in on the conversation that Percy and Jack were having about Jack's fate. Jack looked down and saw his designer clothes had been exchanged for the shabby garb of an anonymous AnCor. Percy was wearing Jack's shoes and Jack wondered who would show up in his pants.

"You're back?" Percy looked at Slash, "How did you get away from the Soldier Police?"

"Greetings, Percy." Slash grinned like a

43

dog who heard his owner getting a leash to walk him. "I'm back."

"Yes. I see that," said Percy, the AnCor camp leader, speaking slowly to be understood by the slow-witted Slash.

Jack simply observed, remaining silent.

"How are you back?" Percy asked as he looked up at his very tall, gangling comrade.

"I'm clever, Percy," Slash bragged. "Got away when they moved me. They was distracted... so, I left. Walked back. So, what's my next assignment?"

"You weren't followed?" Percy checked.

"Nope. Sly. Stayed in shadows, like you taught us," Slash beamed.

Percy handed Slash a photographic device and leaned in to whisper to Slash so that Jack couldn't hear. Then Slash nodded as if he could do the thing that Percy asked of him.

Slash left and returned a few moments later with something to show Percy.

"Very good, Slash," Percy affirmed as he adjusted the loose fitted clothing over his short wiry body with quick nervous energy.

"One day I wanna be as real smart as you are, Percy." Slash's admiration was genuine, his words whistling through the spaces of his missing teeth.

"Thanks," Percy said dismissing the compliment as if it came far too frequently from Slash. "Now, boot up the redmail."

"Right away, Mr. Snatcher," Slash smiled, pleased with himself.

Silently, Jack craned his neck to try and see what it was that Percy and Slash were so proud of.

Then, it dropped to the floor and floated in Jack's direction. He couldn't stop staring at it.

It was a photograph.

Slash scrambled to get it out of Jack's view. It was a picture of Jack on the train after he'd been shot. He was on his back in a pool of his own blood, looking quite dead.

Percy strode over to Jack, "So, now you know."

"Does it matter?" Jack replied nonchalantly.

"He couldn't have figured it out. Percy, I didn't say nothing," Slash protested.

"He knows. He's quick," Percy shot over his shoulder to Slash as he kept his eyes locked onto Jack. "Tell him, Jack. Tell Slash what you think is going on."

Jack remained quiet.

Percy punched him in his wound, "Tell him, Jack. You're a business man. Big powerful head of the big powerful corporation. Educate Slash."

When Percy saw Jack looking into his eyes challengingly, unblinking, silent, Percy grabbed his handgun and cocked it at Jack's head. "You work for me, now, Jack. This is your first order. Tell Slash."

Jack, with jaw clenched, followed

Percy's direction and locked eyes with Slash, "He called my brother Skipper. Skipper won't pay unless I'm dead. That photograph is proof that I'm dead. So, he will make Skipper pay for me. Then, he is going to sell me at the next slave auction and make money on me twice over. That's why he replaced my clothes with these. He is either going to sell or keep my clothes. Your Percy Snatcher is going to squeeze out every credit he possibly can."

"And by doing that," Percy prompted, "it makes up for the fact that we can't sell his Queenie for a profit, right Jack?"

Percy looked for a reaction on Jack's face as he proceeded. "That's right. Your Queenie was killed with the other passengers who weren't important enough to bring us the kind of money we need."

Percy nodded looking at Jack, "Thank you, Corporatist, for explaining to your new boss, Slash." Percy smiled at Slash and said to his co-conspirator, "It will be fun selling a capitalist twice over".

Slash giggled.

"Being a corporatist, a capitalist, a socialist, a communist, or any kind of dictator doesn't matter," Jack shot back, "If the person calling the shots is corrupt, the entire structure is poisoned. Corruption is the decay that makes any organizational system breakdown. I want you to know," Jack stated in his own defense, "I made an effort to be good to my employees. Happy employees make happy customers. I treat my people better than any other corporate leader." Jack took a painful breath through clenched teeth, "Don't confuse me for somebody who doesn't know how to run an organization. I make an effort to be different from the other corporate leaders. I know what is going on in my factories. My employees are respected and well-treated."

"Your factories, their factories," Percy parried, "don't talk to me about how 'different you are'. All factories are the same. Factories work the people 18 hours a day for a bowl of soup, and factory managements give out dirty piles of hay to sleep on. Workers who complain just disappear. The factories demand that our five year old children work on assembly lines. So, it is only right to sell people like you and your class into slavery."

Slash spoke up in the background, "Somebody told me that long ago there were laws that didn't allow kids to work."

"Shut up, Slash," Percy barked.

"My father and I," Jack stated deliberately, "never ran our businesses that way. Other corporate regions have," he acknowledged, "but, I never did and I never would. If you really did your homework on me, you'd know that." Jack took a deep breath, then tried to negotiate, "Look, Mr. Snatcher, I will happily overlook this if you let me walk home. I'll take my chances being wounded and I'll find my own way. I give you my word if you release me now, I won't retaliate."

"Retaliate?" Percy laughed out loud. "Forget it! You are a commodity now and you are going to get me a lot of money."

Percy pushed the button on the redmail machine, sending the photo to Skipper Courtly to confirm that Jack was already dead and the money had better be paid pronto.

Slash laughed. "Brilliant. He is so brilliant," Slash indicated Percy as he talked to Jack.

Just outside the camp perimeter, in the bushes, one Soldier Police skulked. Then a bush moved, revealing another SP. His uniform seemed to automatically camouflage itself to the foliage surrounding him. When he moved in front of a different colored object, his uniform adjusted like a chameleon.

Several miles away in the command center, the cameras worn by each Police Solider sent images that were displayed on a mosaic of screens.

One high-ranking official straightened her jacket, decorated with medals and service-ribbons. She leaned over to the next SP then asked, "Is this where your people followed that man you captured?"

"Affirmative, Ma'am," came the reply of the lower ranking officer.

"The man you let escape was connected to the train attack, correct?" Another gruff highly decorated officer asked the same lower ranking man.

"Affirmative, Sir," was the stiff formal reply. "We knew Officer Gene was on that train as his suit's distress signal indicated, but the AnCors must have deactivated his suit because we lost the signal. We can't even monitor Officer Gene's vitals and don't know if he is dead or alive. However, tracking the escaping AnCor, sir, confirms there is a camp there and intel is 85% certain Officer Gene is in that camp, Sir."

The female officer and male officer looked at each other.

"85%," he said to her.

"Bring that officer home," she replied to him.

"Right," he said as he peered at the multiple screens. "Fly in, number 18," he spoke into a communicator.

At the camp, one Police Soldier responded by silently opening up a small shoe-box labeled #18. Out came a drone disguised as an indigenous dove-like bird. Its eyes were actually camera lenses sending a picture back to command base. The android-bird flew once over the designated camp, giving the high ranking officials a sweeping areal-view of the AnCor bivouac.

From the ground, the drone would appear to have the flapping wings of a genuine living feathered creature. Bird Camera 18 sent back images of AnCors going about their day in this crude garrison: sleeping, eating, playing games, maintaining weapons, just like any other day.

Camera 18 spotted a man, tied outside to a stake, wearing the tatters of a dirty Courtly Corporation Soldier Police uniform. He did not seem conscious. His head was covered in dried blood and dust. No signal was being sent nor received from his uniform.

The gruff man at command center barked into the communicator, "Hold 3 seconds over target."

The aerial bird camera zoomed in on the name badge of the unconscious man, zooming in to one word on his uniform. "Gene". Then, after 3 seconds Camera 18 boomeranged back to its small box #18, and shut down when the SP closed the tiny door.

"The bird is in the nest," the official calmly stated.

At once, stealthy SPs surrounding the camp booted up their sleek laser weapons with a high-pitched whine only canines could detect. Dogs, also clad in the environment-shifting fabric, slowly growled looking to their handlers for the signal.

Each motionless camouflaged SP silently sprang into action, moving with controlled adrenaline. By practiced steps, the SPs avoided treading on dry leaves and twigs, making their approach totally unannounced.

At first, the look-out AnCors on the edge of the perimeter noiselessly dropped. Then, as the Soldier Police circle tightened, more AnCors fell.

One lookout AnCor shouted as he tried to run away, not realizing that he was running toward a wall of more SPs. He yelled once, "Raid!" before dropping to the ground.

The others, some sleeping, some cooking, some playing games, looked up suddenly alert.

One AnCor, snatching up a nearby pistol, shot an oncoming Soldier Police in the chest.

Blended titanium and Kevlar nanoparticles bonded to the fibers of the militant uniforms. The chameleon fabric seemed to react to the bullet upon impact, forming a hard shell like substance within a fraction of a second. The fabric shifted into armored plating at the point of impact, remained for a moment, then faded back into a soft pliable fabric.

The SP's torso felt the impact, but the bullet did not penetrate the fabric of the uniform.

He paused for a moment. While his suit repaired itself, this SP leveled his laser at the shooting AnCor and fired. The rebel fell silently. His comrades, witnessing this, scrambled uselessly away, only to be systematically rounded up, and immobilized.

Three Soldier Police approached their target, the unconscious Officer Gene, guarding him during the takeover. Deftly, they untied the body and wrapped Gene into a blanket of chameleon fabric as they carried him away from the heat of battle.

Upon extraction, the blanket changed colors to match whatever it touched. Any stray debris or ammo that hit the cocooned body, would cause the fabric to harden at the point of impact, protecting the motionless SP.

Slash ran to the small window of the building. He thought he might have heard something.

"Uh, Percy?" Slash said, but by then it was too late.

Percy looked at Slash. "They let you go and then followed you, here! Slash, you led them to our camp!"

"No. No. I checked. Nobody was following me, Percy."

Percy cocked his gun at Slash. Slash, frightened, ran out the door as the shot went off and lodged into the wall. Screams, shouts and shots sounded outside the flimsy structure.

Jack seized this opportunity, and with bound wrists, he attacked Percy.

Percy, having learned street fighting, retaliated with unbridled untrained fury.

Jack's knowledge of the defensive arts evidenced itself with his lithe dodging of Percy's clumsy jabs. In spite of his wounds, Jack fought through the pain. His blows and kicks plowed into Percy's body. Gritting his teeth, Jack focused all his might onto one objective: Get away from these AnCors.

Jack's muscles recalled his rigorous training without having to think. Attack his opponent with three moves, then breathe, then three different moves, so the opponent doesn't have a chance to recover.

Jack continued to push on through his own pain, happy his legs had been left untied. He was thirsty. Tired. Hungry. Aching. But, he had to keep going. He didn't know who was raiding the camp, but knew it was somebody the AnCors were afraid of and he had to use the cover of the attack to get away himself.

With one almost lucky twist of fate, Jack scissor-kicked Percy, causing the AnCor leader to fall backwards and strike his head, rendering him unconscious.

Without taking the time to check if Percy was completely blacked out, Jack snatched the photo of himself from the desk on which it lay, then dashed out the door, tearing the photo into unrecognizable shreds which scattered in the wind as he ran with all the other

AnCors for the camp perimeter.

When Jack realized it was Courtly Soldier Police attacking, he was relieved and stopped running, smiling at one of them, about to call him over for assistance.

Then, the SP who saw him punched a button on his handheld device. Out shot a laser, which hit Jack, paralyzing his muscles. His limbs were unresponsive to Jack's instinct to assume a defensive position. He sank to the ground, unable to even speak, hearing the pandemonium of bullets, shouting, thuds of bodies dropping to the ground...and then Jack heard nothing.

7 CHAPTER Year 2036: A Dancing Date (Continuous Ch 32)

Inside the crowded café, Bjorn and Sarah sat at their tiny table, next to the small dance floor. It was a themed songs night and another old fashioned tune started to play.

Sarah tingled with delight, pleased to be wearing her seldom used fancy dress and her one pair of special shoes. They were the same pair she had worn to Library six years earlier on the day she met Bjorn.

Her outfit was more formal than something she would wear to work, but

59

her look was perfectly suited to gently convey a romantic message to Bjorn.

Sarah accepted Bjorn's extended hand and slight bow as an invitation to dance.

"How many years has it been since I first met you? Five? Six? You never talk about what you did when you were gone, yet..." Sarah teased as they made their way past the other couples. They found an open spot on the dance floor, "...yet you always surprise me with the varied repertoire of skills you've mastered, like partner-dancing to music, Bjorn."

Bjorn's silent reply was to simply draw her closer to him.

After a moment, he grinned and murmured, "Who could forget blueberry-blueberry-pancake? Left-right-left, Left-right-left, Left-right. And repeat." He spoke into her ear to be heard over the music.

"For me it would be right-left-right, wouldn't it?" she retorted playfully.

"Of course," Bjorn spoke as he spun Sarah out and then twirled her return to him, again. He slipped his hand around to the center of her back as he led her to the music. He asked Sarah, "Did you get that thing from the office?"

"Wasn't a problem. Turns out its public knowledge. Not a secret. I have a copy of it in my purse."

"What does it say?" he asked.

"Basically, it just said Skipper had a younger brother named Jack. Even though he was younger, Papa Courtly put Jack, but definitely not Skipper, in charge of Courtly Dynamics Corporation. Then, when Jack and his family died in a tragic train accident, Skipper took charge."

"I'll bet he got rid of anybody loyal to Jack."

"Well, he did get rid of a lot of employees, then hired a bunch more.

61

But, the documents don't describe who was loyal to whom," Sarah explained.

At that moment the song ended and together they walked back to their two-top table and sat down to partake of some refreshing hydration.

Bjorn put his beverage down and asked, "I wonder when the lawyer that you talked to, Mr. Atsushi, became a full time staff attorney? How long has he known the Courtlys?"

"Now why would a reporter covering a simple remodeling story be concerned about all this other stuff?" Sarah leaned toward him, waiting for him to explain.

8 CHAPTER- What will happen next?

The passengers on the train are attacked and slain, dumped into a shallow grave. Will the bodies be discovered and will the AnCors pay for the mayhem they are sowing?

We can assume that Guard Gene was added to the train to make sure the Courtly family was safe, yet he gets shot unexpectedly so he is not able to render any help to the Courtly family at all. Does he witness Jack Courtly taking a bullet for Noah Lantz? Will Guard Gene live through the ordeal?

We catch a glimpse into the events which precipitated Jack Courtly's family vacation. Are there more sinister motives afoot?

In the year 2036, we see that Sarah, now working at Courtly Headquarters for the summer, is asked to do something.

In the year 2030, Slash finds his way back to AnCor camp and finds Percy Snatcher.

℘ To Be Continued... ℘

9 Did You Know

The United States Post office started in 1775 during the Second Continental Congress, where Benjamin Franklin was appointed the first postmaster general. Sarah Paradise shares this information with students on the intern tour.

The US Post office was explicitly authorized in our Constitution to serve all residents, not just a select elite few.

Make a list of other public services. How would society be impacted if all of those public services were denied to the public, and only reserved for a special few?

Do you think that since the post office was placed in our Constitution by the founding fathers of the United States of America, that they must have thought that it was of essential importance?

The American Constitution states "To establish Post Offices and post Roads;" This may have been stipulated in the Constitution because the Founding Fathers had bad experiences with the British postal system. Perhaps it was too expensive for an ordinary person to send a letter. Perhaps deliveries were only able to be sent by the wealthy who had personal servants dedicated to pleasing only their masters.

Before 1765, sending a letter across England cost a week's wages for most people. It was too expensive to send a letter. Can you imagine taking one whole week's salary to splurge on sending just one birthday card? If you sent out 52 Christmas cards, it would take your entire annual salary! And if the weather is bad, the mail simply wasn't delivered at all, and you didn't get a refund.

As the public, shouldn't we support our fire stations? Our libraries? Our water services? Our pre and post offices? Etc.

How would our country function if we did not have any of these services?

Commericalization means charging a fee for a service so that the group providing the service earns a profit. If we commercialized every public service, would those services only become available to the elite few?

Would those services become excessively expensive for everyone else and then finally not be used anymore?

.

ABOUT Wynter Sommers

Wynter Sommers is the pseudonym for an American writing team, which harnesses multiple skills in technology, research, and education. Formally trained with a PhD in Education, Wynter Sommers blends academic classroom experience, with corporate sophistication, and a passion for developing more effective student insights.

Wynter Sommers has taught classrooms of enthusiastic children. She has a heart to inspire creativity and develop critical thinking skills, all to encourage students to make wise choices in life. She wants to impart the talent of honing one's skills in self-reliance and collaborative team work, despite any environmental barriers outside of an individual's control, Wynter Sommers wishes to impart the message that genuine hope, love, and peace can help us overcome obstacles, and cement friendships. Wynter Sommers hopes you enjoy the other *Bjorn Esterday Was not Born Yesterday* stories in this series.

www.ingramcontent.com/pod-product-compliance
Lightning Source LLC
Chambersburg PA
CBHW051841020726
47502CB00005B/1908